The Place of
the Rising Sun

Mr. Tortoise's
Deep River Bank

Mr. Owls
Tall, Tall Tree

Mrs. Rabbit's
Burrow

Mr. Bear's
Deep Dark Cave

For my beautiful girls—Adriana
and Elizabeth—may you always
find your way... Love Mom –A.B.

For Sarah, Derick, Grace, Rachel and
Elsie—may you follow your heart to
find all things exciting, adventurous,
and wonderful...Love Mom –C.B.

Finnigin, a young fisher looking for adventure, wanders too far from home
and finds himself lost. With the help of a twinkling star and some new friends,
Finnigin learns everything he ever wanted was right where he started... home.

ISBN 978-0-9800405-0-0
Library of Congress Control Number: 2007907809

Printed in Mexico
This book was typeset in Palatino.
Illustrations were created using oil pastel, ink and colored pencil.
Thanks from the heart to Doug Berg, Dave and Judy Johnson, Joyce Daugherty,
Red Dirt Studios, Carl Freund, Kandi Johnson and Susan Bocht.

TumbleRock Press ★ www.tumblerockpress.com

5 4 3 2 1

Finnigin
and the Star Jar

Wishing you a twinkling star to always light your way!

April Berg

Christine Berg ★ Illustrated by April Berg

TUMBLEROCK PRESS

Once upon a time there was a very adventurous fisher.
Fishers are adventurous by nature, but Finnigin
was the most adventurous of them all.
Finnigin lived with his large family in a hollow in a
huge fisher tree. Old, huge, and hollow is the best
kind of home for a fisher.
Bright and early one summer morning,
Finnigin especially had a yearning to
explore. He had an itch to
wander and the imagination
to take him far, far away.

Finnigin was on a journey to see how many dragonflies he could catch in one day. So, smitten with the idea, he grabbed his dragonfly jar and started out on his journey. The big dragonfly adventure had begun.

First thing, Finnigin came upon a friendly but sleepy family of possums. "Can you tell me the best place to find as many dragonflies as my dragonfly jar will hold?"

Mother possum pointed Finnigin in a far off direction, toward the place of the rising sun, where the sun rises and greets the day.

Finnigin ventured farther and farther away from the possum family and farther and farther away from the huge and hollow fisher tree and his large fisher family.

Finnigin ran and roamed. He ducked and hid. He jumped and pounced on his journey, and yet, not one dragonfly crossed his path.

Finnigin's tummy started to rumble. His head started to feel a little ache. He was hungry, and he was missing his family and his home.

Finnigin turned around to look behind him, and he was confused. The sun was now setting in the opposite direction. It was evening, and the sun was going down. Finnigin had gone too far. He did not know his way home.

As it grew darker, Finnigin climbed a tall tree to see if
he could find anything familiar. He sat sadly in the
Tall Tall Tree. Night's first star twinkled high above him.
"If only I knew my way. If only I had the light to take me
home." Finnigin began to cry.

As his heart sank, the twinkling star, as if hearing his plea, fell right into his dragonfly jar. Finnigin put the lid tightly on the jar. Now, he had the light to see! Now, it was his star jar. Finnigin jumped with glee.

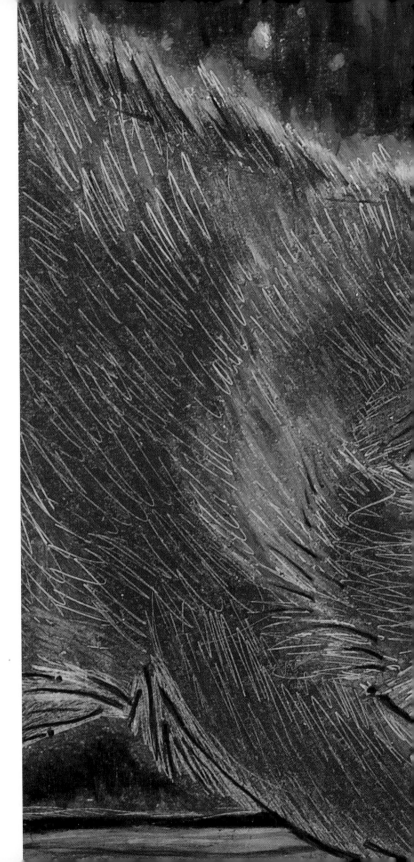

Just as he turned to scurry down the Tall, Tall Tree, huge Mr. Owl swooped down and landed right next to him. "Mr. Owl, you look so wise. Could you please tell me how to get to the huge, hollow fisher tree?"

"Which fisher tree could it be? Could it be the huge, hollow tree that bends and sways over the Willowy Billowy River, around the bend, toward the place where the sun always sets, the land of many fireflies?"

"Yes, Mr. Owl. Yes!"

"Whoo, I do not know the direction now. The sun has gone down. Why don't you go to the Deep, Dark Cave and ask Mr. Bear? I will take you there."

So, off went Finnigin and wise Mr. Owl, using the star jar as their guide, to the Deep, Dark Cave to find Mr. Bear.

"Hellooo," Mr. Owl whooed. "Do you know how to get to the fisher tree?"

"What fisher tree would that be?" growled Mr. Bear. "Could it be the huge, hollow tree that bends and sways over the Willowy Billowy River, around the bend, toward the place where the sun always sets, the land of many fireflies?"

"Yes!" exclaimed an excited Finnigin.

"Do you know how to get there from your deep, dark cave?"

"No, I do not. But, I do know that there is the very intelligent Mrs. Rabbit who knows many, many things and always gives me wise counsel. Maybe she would know. I can take you to her burrow."

So, off they went—wise old owl, burly bear, and a somewhat frightened Finnigin, using the star jar to light their way.

Soon, they came upon Mrs. Rabbit's Burrow. Mrs. Rabbit, who was tucking in her little ones for the night, welcomed them to her home.

"What can I do for you, kind Mr. Bear?" Mrs. Rabbit asked.

"We are looking for the fisher tree. Young Finnigin has lost his way," replied Mr. Bear.

"Which fisher tree could it be? Could it be the huge, hollow tree that houses the large fisher family? The one that bends and sways over the Willowy Billowy River, around the bend, toward the place where the sun always sets, the land of many fireflies?"

"Yes! Yes, that's it!" Finnigin bounced up and down excitedly. "Do you know how to get there from here?"

"I'm afraid I do not know, not at this time of night, but your mother and father must be worried so. I know of a wise Mr. Tortoise. He knows the Willowy Billowy River. I presume that he can take us there. Follow me. I will show you the way to Mr. Tortoise's lair. I will bring you there."

So, on they went—the owl, the bear, the rabbit, and the fisher through tall grasses and swampy bogs to the Deep River Bank where Mr. Tortoise was just making his bed.

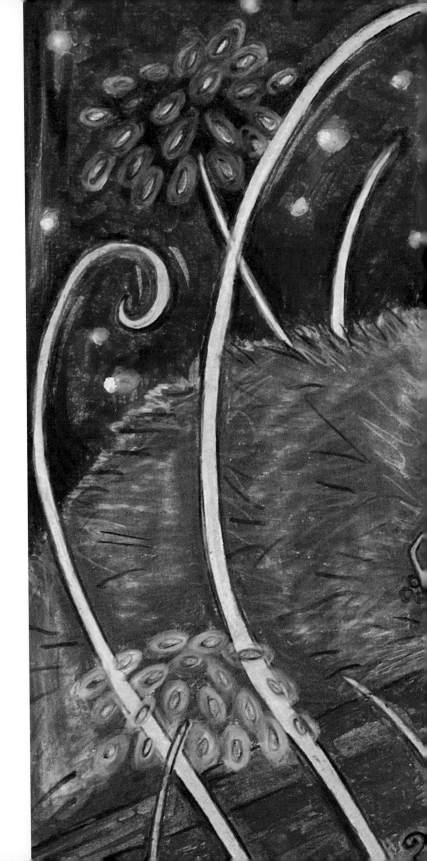

"Mr. Tortoise," called Mrs. Rabbit. "Do you have a moment?"

"Yes, Mrs. Rabbit, for you I have all the time in the world, my friend."

Mrs. Rabbit went on, "This young fisher is so very lost. He cannot find his home—the great fisher tree. Could you possibly show him the way?"

"Now, which fisher tree could this great fisher tree be?" replied Mr. Tortoise.

Finnigin was sad, discouraged, cold, and hungry. "It is the Great Fisher Tree. The home of my large fisher family. It is the huge, hollow tree that bends and sways over the Willowy Billowy River, around the big, snarly, gnarly bend, toward the place where the sun always sets, the land of many fireflies."

"I know the place," yawned slow Mr. Tortoise.
"I could take you there if I only had a light."

"I have a light!" shouted the emphatic young
Finnigin. "My star jar. Here! See?"

"Just climb upon my back, friends, and I will lead
you home."

So they climbed on Mr. Tortoise's back, except for
Mr. Bear, who followed along the bank, and Mr. Owl,
who flew close by.

Away he swam. Away they floated down the
Willowy Billowy River with Finnigin holding out
his star jar to light the way in the deep, dark night.

Slush, slosh. The water sounded as Mr. Tortoise made his way to the bend of the great Willowy Billowy River. On they went, until suddenly—there it was in plain view—the snarly, gnarly bend. On the other side, Finnigin had never seen such a sight. He was home!

He could see the tree and his family there waiting for him. Finnigin had never been so happy. There, in front of his home, were hundreds of fireflies—blinking little lights—more than he had ever seen before or more than he had ever noticed.

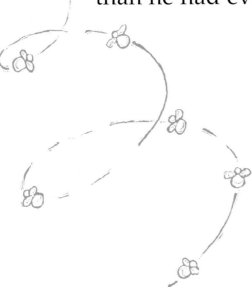

Finnigin hopped off Mr. Tortoise's back and ran up to his family. They hugged, laughed, smiled, and cried as Finnigin told about all of his adventures and how he had wandered so far from home looking for something exciting, adventurous, and wonderful.

Finnigin realized that everything he ever wanted was right here on the Willowy Billowy River in the huge, hollow tree. Finnigin had as many fireflies as his star jar could possibly hold. He had his wonderful family, and he was happy. He was where he should be. Finnigin was home.

The End

A Journey Home

The Place
Where the Sun
Always Sets

The Great
Fisher Tree

The Willowy Billowy River

The Land of
Many Fireflies